Blackout

BY ANNE & HARLOW ROCKWELL

Macmillan Publishing Co., Inc.

New York

Macmillan Publishing Co., Inc.
866 Third Avenue, New York, N.Y. 10022
Collier Macmillan Canada, Ltd.
Printed in the United States of America
10 9 8 7 6 5 4 3 2 1

Library of Congress Cataloging in Publication Data
Rockwell, Anne F   Blackout.
Summary: Dan and his family face hardship and danger when
an ice storm causes a 3-day power failure in their town.
[1. Natural disasters—Fiction.   2. Survival—Fiction]
I. Rockwell, Harlow, joint author.   II. Title.
PZ7.R5943Bl   [E]   78-12185   ISBN 0-02-777610-7

For
Hannah,
Elizabeth,
Oliver
and Wimpy

CHAPTER ONE

It was cold.

All the trees

were covered with ice.

Every branch of every tree

was shining with ice.

"Oh, how pretty

the trees look!" said Dan.

"Yes, they do," said Father.
"But I hope the wind
   does not begin to blow."
The wind began to blow.
The ice began to crack.
The branches began to break.

CRASH!

One big branch fell down.

CRASH!

Another fell down.

The wind blew harder.

CRASH! CRASH!

The television went off.

So did the light

in the bathroom.

CHAPTER TWO

"Look," said Mother.
"An electric power line
is down.
That is why
the light went out.
And the television, too."

Timmy began to cry.

His favorite cartoon

was gone.

Dan looked out the window.

He shouted,

"Sparks are coming

out of that wire!"

And they were.
Father telephoned
the power company.
"Our lights are out,"
he said.
"There is a live wire
making sparks on our street.
There are dogs and cats
and little children
on our street.
Please hurry
and fix the live wire
before someone gets hurt."

The person
at the power company said,
"We will fix
the live wire right away.
That is an emergency.
We will try to turn on
your electric power
at the same time.
But power lines
are being knocked down
all over town.
We will do our best."

Dan and Timmy and Tugger
sat at the window
and watched the sparks
coming from the broken wire.
The furnace went off
and the house
began to get cold.
Dan began to shiver.

Father built a fire
in the fireplace.
He used the wood
Grandmother had given
them for Christmas.
Dan was glad
they had a fire.
It was nice and warm.
It was pretty, too.

CHAPTER THREE

A truck from
the power company came.
The workers turned off
the power from the utility pole.

No more sparks came
from the wire.
But they could not fix
the broken wire right away.
They had to take care of
other live wires
on other streets.
"We will be back,"
they said.
But night came.
They did not come back.

Father called the power company.
Mother did, too.
But the line was always busy.
The wind blew.
The branches cracked.
And the house was cold
and dark,
except by the fireplace.
"We can cook over the fire,"
said Mother.
And they did.

There were hot dogs,
marshmallows and popcorn.
"This is fun," said Dan.
"It is like a picnic."
"It is fun right now,"
said Father.
"But I hope they fix
the electric power soon."

"It is too dark to eat,"

said Mother.

She found two candles.

She lit them

and they had light

to eat by.

Father and Dan
took a flashlight
and found the sleeping bags
in the attic.

Each of them put on
three pairs of socks.
"This is like the North Pole,"
said Dan.

Then Father found
the portable radio.
It worked with batteries.
Everyone listened to the news.
The radio announcer
told them what to do
during the blackout.

Father went down
to the cellar.

Mother went into the kitchen.

She turned on the faucet
in the sink.

She filled big pots
with water.

Then she left the water running.

She went into the bathroom.

She turned on the faucets

in the sink and the tub.

She flushed the toilet.

She left all the faucets running.

Father turned off

the water valve in the cellar.

Soon all the faucets

stopped running.

"Now," said Father,
"there is no more water
in our pipes.
So our pipes cannot freeze."

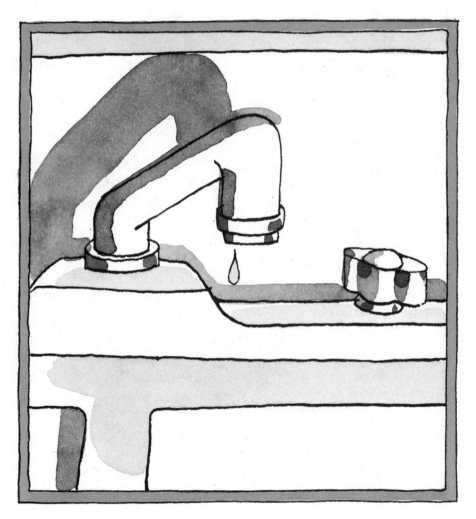

They each got into
a sleeping bag.

Then Dan thought of something.

"My goldfish!" he said.

He put his goldfish bowl

on the bookcase

by the fireplace.

"Now my goldfish

will not turn to ice,"

he said.

"My plants!" said Mother.
She brought her plants
down from the bedroom.
She put them next to
the goldfish.
"Now they will not freeze,"
she said.

Tugger snuggled up
with Timmy.
He began to whimper.
Timmy held him tight.

The wind blew.

A branch fell on the roof.

Ice cracked.

Father put more wood

on the fire.

Everyone told stories

and jokes

and sang songs

until they fell asleep.

More ice cracked

and the wind blew.

CHAPTER FOUR

When they woke up,
the wind had stopped.
But it was cold.
Ice still covered the trees.
All day everyone waited
for the power to go on.
All day there was a warm fire
in the fireplace.
By three o'clock,
there was no more wood.
There were no more candles.

Dan walked to the store.

It was dark in the store.

People with shopping carts

were bumping into each other.

The electric cash registers
did not work.
The clerks had to add
with pencils and paper.
Dan bought one box of candles.
That was all he could find.

When he got home,
Mother said,
"We have called
all the places that sell wood
that are nearby.
No one has any.
But I know an old farm
where they sell wood.
It is not in the telephone book.
I will drive there
and try to buy some wood."

But Father said,
"No, I will go.
The roads are icy
and it is dangerous to drive.
I will go."

"No," said Mother.

"You do not know the way.
You would just get lost.
You can stay here
with Timmy and Tugger.
Dan can help me.
And just you wait and see!
When we get home,
the lights will be on.
The furnace will be on.
The house will be
nice and warm.
And we can save the wood
for next winter."

CHAPTER FIVE

The roads were icy.
The car skidded.
It amost skidded
off the road.

Dan saw many, many
broken power lines.
In one place, a big tree
lay across the road.
Broken power lines
were twisted
in its branches.

"Now we will have to go

the back way," said Mother.

"I did not want to go

up the hill on this ice.

But we must get wood

or we will freeze."

The hill was steep and icy.

But the car did not skid.

"Wow!" said Mother,

as they got to the old farm.

"I was scared!

Weren't you?"

"Yes," said Dan.

"I was scared, too."

There was not much wood
to buy at the old farm.
Mother bought all they had.

As they drove home,

it began to get dark.

"This wood will last all night,"

said Dan.

"But we will be cold tomorrow."

They passed a truck.

Workers were fixing

a power line.

"They will fix ours soon,"

said Mother.

CHAPTER SIX

That night they had
canned beans,
canned tuna fish,
crackers and cookies
and water from the pots
in the kitchen.

There was ice on top of
the water in the pots.
When Dan went to the bathroom,
he could not flush the toilet.
He could not wash his hands
or brush his teeth.
And it was icy cold
in the bathroom.
They all got into sleeping bags.
They listened to the radio.
Suddenly the radio was quiet.
The batteries were used up.

"I will find some batteries,"
said Dan.

He found two good batteries
in his racing car.

He put them in the radio.

But the news was just the same
as the night before.

Dan felt scared.

Now he did not like the dark.

He did not like the cold.

Timmy cried because
now he wanted to sleep
in his own bed.

So Mother sang
"Old MacDonald Had a Farm."
That always made Timmy laugh.
Father told three
knock-knock jokes.
And then Dan told
knock-knock jokes, too.
Mother told a long story.
Dan, Timmy, Tugger,
Mother and Father
all watched the sparks
and flames of the fire.

Late that night,

there was a knock

at the door.

It was a neighbor.

He had no more wood.

Father gave him

some of theirs.

And before the sun came up,

all their wood was gone.

CHAPTER SEVEN

In the morning,
it was not as cold.
The ice began to melt
in the sun.

Dan said,
"We have one candle,
two radio batteries,
one flashlight
and no wood.
What will we do tonight?"
"Shhh," said Father.
"Let's listen to the radio.
Maybe they will tell us
where to go to keep warm."
But suddenly the radio
was quiet again.
The last good batteries
were all used up.

All day they waited.

The ice dripped and melted

in the sunshine.

Then the sun went down.

It began to get darker

and colder.

Suddenly, as the stars came out,

a truck came.

A truck from the power company!

"Hooray!" shouted Dan.

"Wow!" said Timmy,

when he saw the lights

on the truck.

"We sure are glad to see you,"
said Mother and Father
and all the neighbors
to the workers on the truck.
They worked hard and fast.
In a little while, the lights
in all the houses went on.

Father switched on the furnace.
"Soon the house will be warm,"
he said.
He turned on the water valve
in the cellar.
Mother turned off the faucets
as the water began to run.
She turned on the stove
and made hot coffee
for the workers from
the power company.
Timmy turned on the television.
A sports car race was on.
Timmy liked that.

Dan turned on the light
in his room.
It was still cold,
but he could hear noises
coming from the radiator.
Nice noises!

Soon it would get warm.
Dan lay down on his own bed
and finished his book
about dinosaurs.
Tugger ran around barking
and chasing his tail
because he was so happy.
The blackout was over.

Ready for fun?

Don't miss READY-TO-READ HANDBOOKS like these.

IT'S MAGIC?
Written and illustrated by Robert Lopshire

"Fourteen fool-proof tricks requiring little practice and utilizing readily available material, explained in brief, easy-to-read text and explicit cartoonlike drawings."—*A.L.A. Booklist*

"...a sure way to mystify friends and entertain parents."
—*Kirkus Reviews*

DECEMBER DECORATIONS
By Peggy Parish / Illustrated by Barbara Wolff

Thirty Christmas and Chanukah decorations children can make all by themselves, "explained separately and simply for the youngest reader. ...Illustrations in green and black do a good job of explaining steps."
—*A.L.A. Booklist*

I DID IT
Written and illustrated by Harlow Rockwell

"Four children describe, in first-person narrative, their methods for making a paper-bag mask, a bean-and-seed picture, a papier-maché fish, a paper airplane, invisible ink, and simple yeast bread....this book's unusual approach...lends itself readily to independent work by young children."—*A.L.A. Booklist*

YOUR FIRST PET
By Carla Stevens / Illustrated by Lisl Weil

"A pet care book that primary graders can read themselves. Short chapters describe the housing, feeding, and taming or training of gerbils, hamsters, mice, guinea pigs, goldfish, parakeets, kittens, and puppies. ...gives enough information for children to get started and adds important hints."—*A.L.A. Booklist*

"Parents...could do worse than make [this] book a required pre-requisite to that first pet shop purchase."—*Kirkus Reviews*

EVENING GRAY, MORNING RED
Written and illustrated by Barbara Wolff

"Primary graders are pleasantly introduced to weather through simple rhymes about clouds, sky color, the sun and moon, animals and birds, plants, and wind. Each selection is accompanied by a factual explanation of the scientific theory on which the rhyme is based."
—*School Library Journal*

"An informal, entertaining invitation to the subject."—*A.L.A. Booklist*